MAKE EVERY DAY EARTH DAY!

CARING FOR OUR PLANET

By VITA JIMÉNEZ
Illustrations by GEORGE ERMOS
Music by DREW TEMPERANTE

CANTATA LEARNING

WWW.CANTATALEARNING.COM

CANTATA
LEARNING

Published by Cantata Learning
1710 Roe Crest Drive
North Mankato, MN 56003
www.cantatalearning.com

A note to educators and librarians from the publisher: Cantata Learning has provided the following data to assist in book processing and suggested use of Cantata Learning product.

Publisher's Cataloging-in-Publication Data
Prepared by Librarian Consultant: Ann-Marie Begnaud
Library of Congress Control Number: 2016938061
Make Every Day Earth Day! : Caring for Our Planet
Series: Me, My Friends, My Community : Caring for Our Planet
By Vita Jiménez
Illustrations by George Ermos
Music by Drew Temperante
Summary: In this catchy song paired with colorful illustrations, children learn how to care for our planet.
ISBN: 978-1-63290-783-7 (library binding/CD)
ISBN: 978-1-68410-105-4 (paperback)
Suggested Dewey and Subject Headings:
Dewey: E 394.262
LCSH Subject Headings: Earth Day – Juvenile literature. | Environmental responsibility – Juvenile literature. | Earth Day – Songs and music – Texts. | Environmental responsibility – Songs and music – Texts. | Earth Day – Juvenile sound recordings. | Environmental responsibility – Juvenile sound recordings.
Sears Subject Headings: Environmental protection. | School songbooks. | Children's music. | Popular music.
BISAC Subject Headings: JUVENILE NONFICTION / Science & Nature / Environmental Conservation & Protection. | JUVENILE NONFICTION / Music / Songbooks. | JUVENILE NONFICTION / Holidays & Celebrations / Other, Non-Religious.

Book design and art direction: Tim Palin Creative
Editorial direction: Flat Sole Studio
Music direction: Elizabeth Draper
Music written and produced by Drew Temperante

Printed in the United States of America in North Mankato, Minnesota.
072017 0367CGF17

TIPS TO SUPPORT LITERACY AT HOME

WHY READING AND SINGING WITH YOUR CHILD IS SO IMPORTANT

Daily reading with your child leads to increased academic achievement. Music and songs, specifically rhyming songs, are a fun and easy way to build early literacy and language development. Music skills correlate significantly with both phonological awareness and reading development. Singing helps build vocabulary and speech development. And reading and appreciating music together is a wonderful way to strengthen your relationship.

READ AND SING EVERY DAY!

TIPS FOR USING CANTATA LEARNING BOOKS AND SONGS DURING YOUR DAILY STORY TIME

1. As you sing and read, point out the different words on the page that rhyme. Suggest other words that rhyme.
2. Memorize simple rhymes such as Itsy Bitsy Spider and sing them together. This encourages comprehension skills and early literacy skills.
3. Use the questions in the back of each book to guide your singing and storytelling.
4. Read the included sheet music with your child while you listen to the song. How do the music notes correlate to the words of the song?
5. Sing along on the go and at home. Access music by scanning the QR code on each Cantata book. You can also stream or download the music for free to your computer, smartphone, or mobile device.

Devoting time to daily reading shows that you are available for your child. Together, you are building language, literacy, and listening skills.

Have fun reading and singing!

On Earth Day, we are reminded to take care of the Earth. People all over the world celebrate Earth Day each year on April 22. On that day, people plant trees, clean up **trash** in parks and on beaches, and do other things to help our **environment**. But Earth Day doesn't need to be just one day. We can help our Earth all year long!

Now turn the page and sing along!

APRIL
22
EARTH
DAY

On Earth Day, we work together
to help animals, land, oceans, and air.
But we can do things every day
to save our planet and show we care.

Plants and animals live all over our planet:
in the water, on land, and underground.
Let's keep their **habitats** nice and safe.
They'll have a better chance of staying around!

Trees give us food, wood, and animal homes.
Trees give us paper and **oxygen** too!
Trees are important for all living things.
Let's plant a tree. Plant a tree or two!

On Earth Day, we work together
to help animals, land, oceans, and air.
But we can do things every day
to save our planet and show we care.

All living things need clean water,
so we need to keep rivers and oceans clean.
The things you flush away don't just disappear.
They end up in our lakes and streams.

RAIN

Let's work together and not waste water.
We need clean water to drink and wash our clothes.
Save water by taking short showers.
Let rain water the yard instead of a hose.

We all need clean air to breathe,
but exhaust from cars causes **pollution**,
so take a walk or ride a bike.
We can skip the trip to a gas station.

SCHOOL

On Earth Day, we work together
to help animals, land, oceans, and air.
But we can do things every day
to save our planet and show we care.

SONG LYRICS

Make Every Day Earth Day!

On Earth Day, we work together
to help animals, land, oceans, and air.
But we can do things every day
to save our planet and show we care.

Plants and animals live all over our planet:
in the water, on land, and underground.
Let's keep their habitats nice and safe.
They'll have a better chance of staying around!

Trees give us food, wood, and animal homes.
Trees give us paper and oxygen too!
Trees are important for all living things.
Let's plant a tree. Plant a tree or two!

On Earth Day, we work together
to help animals, land, oceans, and air.
But we can do things every day
to save our planet and show we care.

All living things need clean water,
so we need to keep rivers and oceans clean.
The things you flush away don't just disappear.
They end up in our lakes and streams.

Let's work together and not waste water.
We need clean water to drink and wash
our clothes.
Save water by taking short showers.
Let rain water the yard instead of a hose.

We all need clean air to breathe,
but exhaust from cars causes pollution,
so take a walk or ride a bike.
We can skip the trip to a gas station.

On Earth Day, we work together
to help animals, land, oceans, and air.
But we can do things every day
to save our planet and show we care.

Make Every Day Earth Day!

Hip Hop
Drew Temperante

Verse 2
Trees give us food, wood, and animal homes.
Trees give us paper and oxygen too!
Trees are important for all living things.
Let's plant a tree. Plant a tree or two!

Chorus

Verse 3
All living things need clean water,
so we need to keep rivers and oceans clean.
The things you flush away don't just disappear.
They end up in our lakes and streams.

Verse 4
Let's work together and not waste water.
We need clean water to drink and wash our clothes.
Save water by taking short showers.
Let rain water the yard instead of a hose.

Verse 5
We all need clean air to breathe,
but exhaust from cars causes pollution,
so take a walk or ride a bike.
We can skip the trip to a gas station.

Chorus

ACCESS THE MUSIC!
SCAN CODE WITH MOBILE APP
CANTATALEARNING.COM

GLOSSARY

environment—the natural world around us

habitats—the natural places where animals live

oxygen—a colorless gas in the air that people and animals need to breathe

pollution—anything that makes the air, water, or land unclean

trash—things that are no longer useful and are thrown away

GUIDED READING ACTIVITIES

1. Why do you think the author used this title?
2. What is one thing you can do to help celebrate Earth Day?
3. Would you recommend this book to a friend? Why?
4. What do you like most about Earth Day?

TO LEARN MORE

Celia, Clara. *Earth Day*. North Mankato, MN: Capstone, 2013.

Ghigna, Charles. *We Need Water*. North Mankato, MN: Capstone, 2012.

Peschke, Marci. *Green Queen*. North Mankato, MN: Capstone, 2014.

Rissman, Rebecca. *Earth Day*. Chicago, IL: Heinemann-Raintree, 2011.